MW00947304

Happy Bug-Hunting!

Jane Barrell

2018

Hector Visits His Country Cousin

Text By
Jane Scoggins Bauld

Illustrated by
Gary Laronde

EAKIN PRESS Austin, Texas

FIRST EDITION
Copyright © 2002
By Jane Scoggins Bauld
Published in the United States of America
By Eakin Press
A Division of Sunbelt Media, Inc.
P.O. Drawer 90159 🖼 Austin, Texas 78709-0159
email: sales@eakinpress.com
🖳 website: www.eakinpress.com 🖳
ALL RIGHTS RESERVED.
1 2 3 4 5 6 7 8 9
ISBN 1-57168-601-0 HB
     1-57168-676-2 PB

Library of Congress Cataloging-in-Publication Data

Bauld, Jane Scoggins.
    Hector visits his country cousin / text by Jane Scoggins Bauld / illustrated by Gary Laronde.
        p.   cm.
    Summary: Hector, a Mexican free-tailed bat whose home is under Congress Avenue Bridge in Austin, Texas, visits a cousin in Braken Cave.
     ISBN 1-57168-601-0 — ISBN 1-57168-676-2 (pbk : alk. paper)
      1. Bats–Juvenile fiction. [1. Bats–Fiction. 2. Mexican free-tailed bat–Fiction. 3. Austin (Tex.)–Fiction.] I. Laronde, Gary, ill. II. Title.
PZ10.3.B318 He 2002
[E]–dc21   2002003191

This book is dedicated to the memory of Ed Eakin (1927–2002), founder and owner of Eakin Press, whose books that open doors of understanding for children will endure throughout history.

—JANE SCOGGINS BAULD

For my father and mother, Bert and Elizabeth Laronde.

—GARY LARONDE

A Word About Bracken Cave

About 60 miles from Austin, Texas, is the world's largest bat colony. More than 40 million bats live in Bracken Cave.

The cave is owned by Bat Conservation International, an organization that works around the world to protect bats.

Bracken Cave reeks with bat droppings, called "guano." This smell can be harmful to humans, but the bats have adapted to it. Bat guano is used to make fertilizer, insecticides, detergents, and antibiotics.

A Word About Bats

Bats like to be left alone—they like quiet places. But the bats that live under Congress Avenue Bridge in Austin, Texas, have adapted to city life. They sleep right through the noise of the city.

Bats are the only mammals that can fly. Their wings are their arms and hands. Bats judge distance and direction by emitting high-pitched sounds. This is called echolocation.

When bat pups are born, they learn to talk with their mother and to recognize her smell. Each type of bat has its own different calls—one sound for food, another for danger, and another that a mother bat uses to call her pup.

"Get out of here, you little beast!" the secretary shouted, chasing Hector around the office with a long-handled broom.

"Get out of here and stay out!"

Hector was only too glad to oblige! He rushed through the open window, out into the warm freshness of the evening air.

"Whew! That was a close call!" he said to himself.

His mother had cautioned him about office buildings, but he wanted to see what was inside. And besides, he had seen a bug flying around the ceiling light!

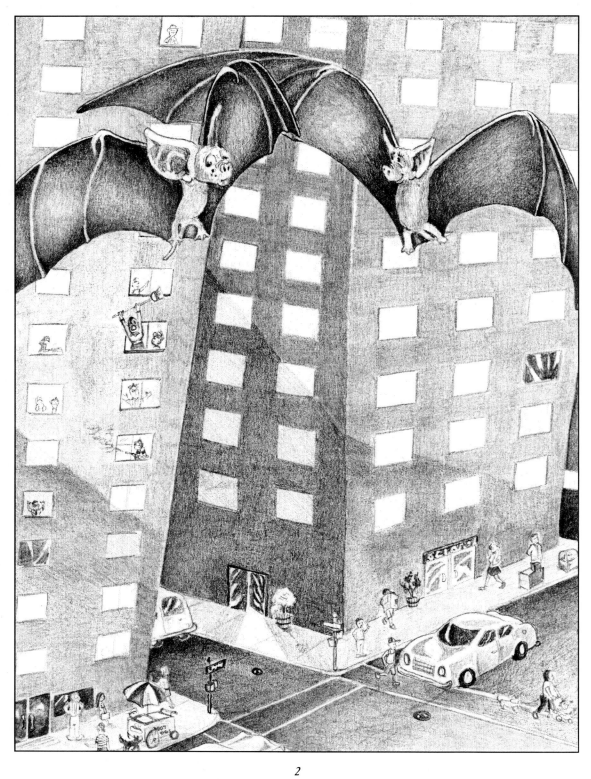

"Hector, please stay out of trouble," his mother pleaded. "And remember what I told you about poisoned bugs. Sometimes the city sprays to kill mosquitoes. Bugs that have been sprayed with poison are poison to you, too!"

Hector always tried to remember the wise advice his mother gave him, but after all, he was just a pup. And a curious pup, at that! He couldn't help it if he wanted to know about things.

"There is so much to explore!" Hector exclaimed.

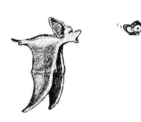

Hector loved the city.

There was always something going on—traffic crossing his Congress Avenue Bridge, horns honking, and sirens wailing.

There was usually music coming from the park beside the river, and children laughing along the banks.

Some nights, as Hector hunted for insects, he gazed at the big stars that spread across the Texas sky.

Some nights, he watched the moon come up over the Texas Capitol.

Hector didn't mind the noise.

That is—until the Fourth of July . . .

That evening, Hector and his mother were later than usual leaving the bridge. It was just after sundown, and they were stretching their wings, ready to fly out to look for bugs.

That was when it began:

BOOM! BOOM! BOOM!

The booms were deafening to Hector's sensitive ears.

"What's going on?" he shouted to his mother.

"It's a celebration, Hector. Let's get out of here. By the time we come back at dawn, the celebration will be over."

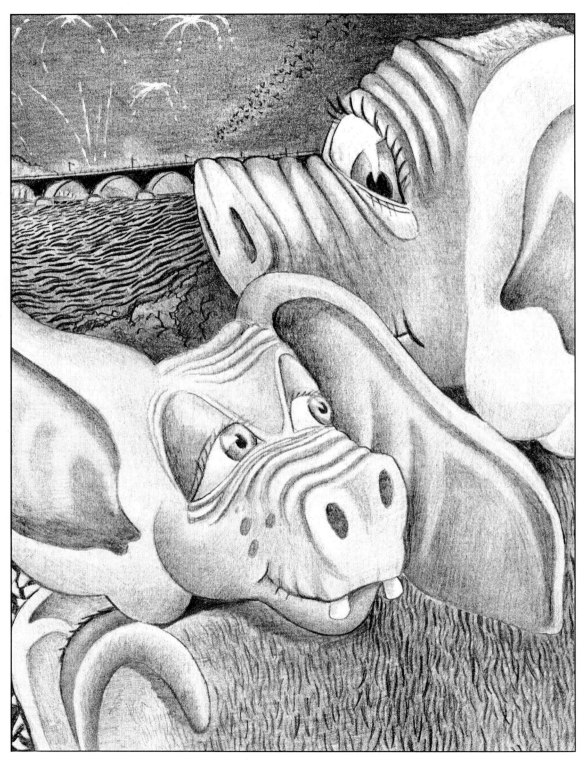

Quickly, they left the bridge.

Hector followed his mother for a while, then, still a bit dizzy from the booms, he decided to spin off on his own.

"I'll go visit Cousin Harvey," he decided.

Mother had told him about Harvey. "Harvey lives in the country, where it is quiet. He lives in a cave."

Hector wondered what a cave was like. Would it be anything like his bridge?

He headed due south. Soon the bright lights of the city were far behind. Hector had never seen it so dark. Could he ever find a bug in the dark?

On he flew, in the direction of Bracken Cave, where Cousin Harvey lived.

Suddenly, he bumped smack into something.

It was Cousin Harvey!

"Hey, watch where you're going!" Harvey scolded. "When you fly in the dark, you have to use echolocation. There's no telling what you might bump into."

Gradually, Hector's eyes became accustomed to the dark. He looked Harvey over. Harvey looked a lot like Hector, with brown velvety fur, wrinkled lips, and glorious wings.

"Come on," Harvey said at last. "Let's play."

Hector and Harvey took off. "How do you find bugs in the dark?" Hector asked.

"Easy. Just listen. Just use your ears—you can hear them flying."

There was complete silence.

The only soft sound Hector heard was the wind blowing through the cottonwood trees.

"Nice," thought Hector. Then he heard something else—the sound of a flying bug!

"Yes!" Hector said as he gobbled up the bug. "I *can* catch bugs in the dark."

Just before dawn, Harvey said, "Come on, Hector. It's time to head home."

Hector followed Harvey straight to Bracken Cave. By sunrise, all the bats who lived in the cave had returned, ready to sleep for the day.

Hector was surprised to see that more bats lived in Harvey's cave than lived under his bridge.

But it was hard for Hector to sleep in such quietness.

There were no city sounds.

There was only deep, black darkness, and deep, dark silence.

Hector dropped off to sleep, feeling a little lonely.

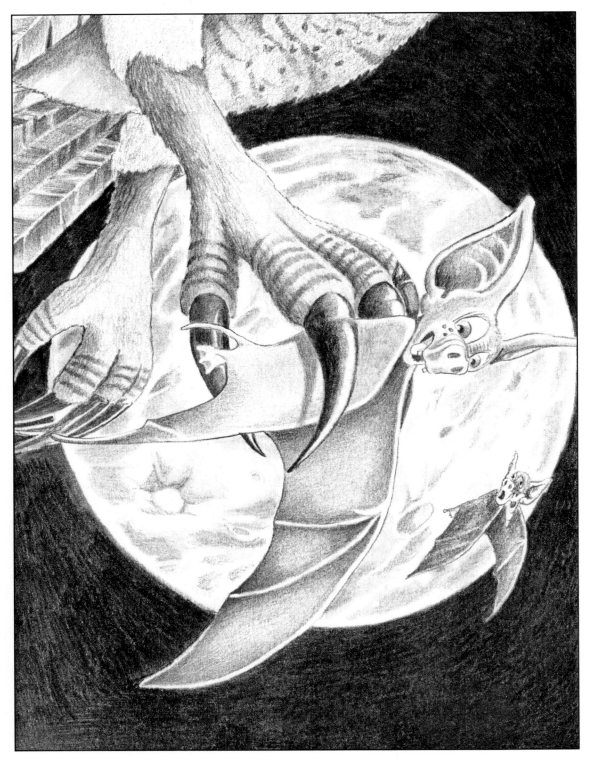

Hector stayed with Cousin Harvey for almost a week.

Each night they had a different adventure.

One night in particular Hector would never forget. His mother had warned him about owls, but he had never actually seen one. Sometimes he thought she was just making them up.

But that night, Hector flew straight into an owl! He was scared out of his wits! He felt the owl's beak clutch his body. He felt the owl's talons clawing at him.

Somehow—he never knew exactly how—he wriggled out of the owl's grasp.

"Whew!" he exclaimed. "That was a close call. There really are owls. I'd better use my echolocation, so I can hear when an owl is nearby."

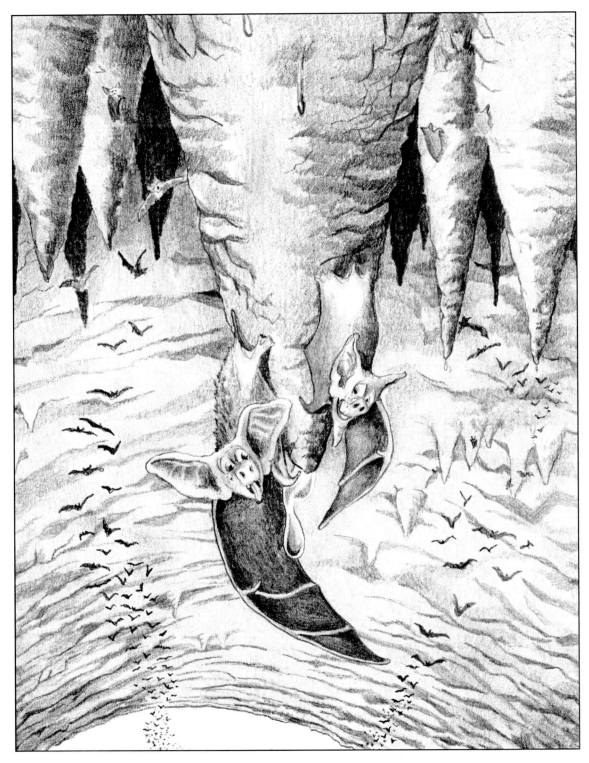

Another night, Hector and Harvey explored an unknown area of the cave. The only sound was that of slow, dripping water from a stalactite.

Each day, Hector slept beside Harvey in Bracken Cave. It was hot in there, with all the millions of bats. Hector missed the cool air of the river.

The smell of guano was strong inside the cave. Hector decidedly did not like it! Some days he moved closer to the entrance, just to get some fresh air.

Hector thought about the river, the children laughing, and the music playing. He thought about the moon coming up over the Texas Capitol.

"Harvey, old Cousin, I think it's time for me to head back home. I miss city life," Hector told him.

"But Hector, can't you live here in the country with me?" Harvey pleaded.

"Oh, no," Hector said. "My place is in the city. That's where I was born. This has been a good visit, but there's no place like home. Good-bye, Cousin Harvey."

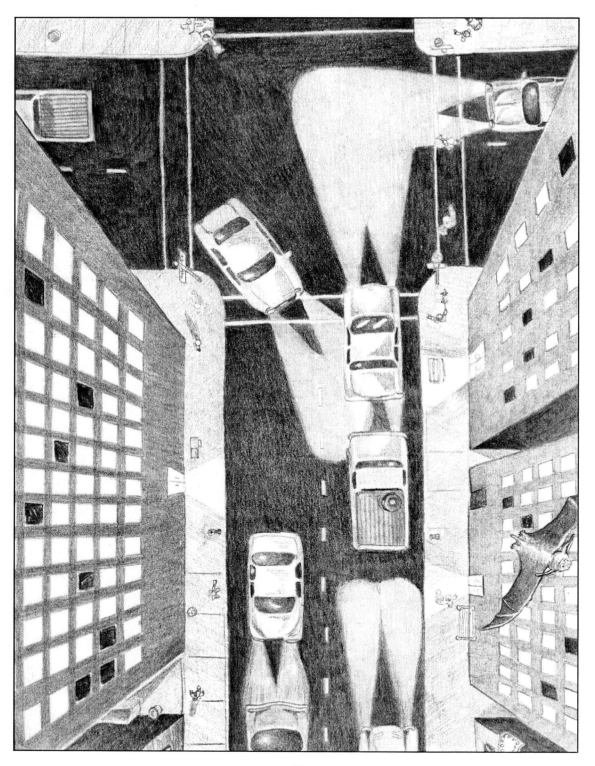

And with that, Hector was off. He spread his wings and caught a high tail wind that helped him along.

On he flew through the dark sky. He caught bugs as he flew. "I have good echolocation!" he declared.

A little before morning, Hector could see the glow of lights from the city. He suddenly realized how much he had missed it.

Confident now in familiar territory, Hector made his way between the tall buildings of the city that soon would be buzzing with activity.

Before long, Hector would hear horns honking, and children laughing, and music playing.

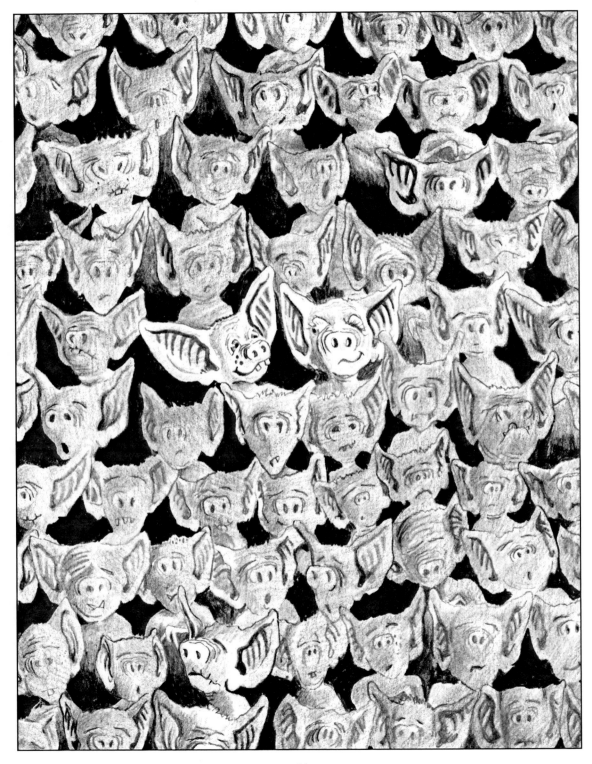

The sight of the bridge made his heart go pitter-pat.

How cool the river air felt to his tired body!

"I'm home," he said to his mother, as he snuggled beside her to sleep. "I'm home."

Hector thought about his country cousin. He remembered how quiet it had been.

Hector breathed a sigh of relief. He was right where he belonged. He might visit Cousin Harvey again, but his home was here—Congress Avenue Bridge, Austin, Texas, 78704.

"There's no place like home," he whispered.

About the Author

After retiring from a 30-year teaching career, **Jane Scoggins Bauld** spends her time writing children's books. She has 17 published books, and makes frequent visits to schools to talk with children about writing and to read her books to them.

Jane primarily loves being with her grandchildren, but she still remains active in her community, serving on the board of directors of several organizations, and presenting writing conferences for the University of Texas, Writers' League of Texas, and the Society of Children's Book Writers and Illustrators.

She lives in Austin with her husband Nathan, their cat Maui, and their dog Quanah.

About the Illustrator

For as long as he can remember, **Gary Laronde** has always loved to draw. He is a self-taught artist who has been influenced by the paintings of Renoir and Rockwell. His interest in illustrating children's books was sparked by watching "Reading Rainbow" with his young sons. Gary currently lives in Arlington, Texas, with his very supportive wife, Minnie, and his two wonderful sons, Brandon and Shane.